Rockets

MRS MAGIC

Magic Hotel

Wendy Smith

A & C Black • London

for Anna and Martin

Rockets

MRS MAGIC – Wendy Smith

Circle Magic
Crazy Magic
Magic Hotel
Mouse Magic

First paperback edition 2000
First published 2000 in hardback by
A & C Black (Publishers) Ltd
35 Bedford Row, London WC1R 4JH

ISBN 0-7136-5328-0

A CIP catalogue record for this book is available
from the British Library.

Printed and bound by G. Z. Printek, Bilbao, Spain.

Chapter One

Mrs Magic ran a hotel.
Not just any hotel.

It was a creepy house in a creepy place. Nearby was the Wild Forest where fierce animals lived.

Puss and Partridge helped Mrs Magic
run the hotel.

All sorts of people came to stay.
Children were Mrs Magic's
favourite guests.

Partridge looked up from his paper.

Outside a coach screeched to a halt.
The school party had arrived.

As soon as they had been let out,
the children rushed to the front door,
followed by Mr Bush their teacher.

Partridge opened the door.

Mrs Magic greeted the children with a
surprise spell.

Chapter Two

When their bags had safely landed, Partridge led everyone up the 2,650 steps to the Tower.

The children were glad to lie down.

They had barely settled in when Puss
banged the gong
for supper.

Down 2,650 steps they went. They
followed Puss through the library.

A secret door opened on to a narrow
staircase. Down, down they went.

In the depths of the dungeon Partridge
served crispy bat-wings and curried
rat-tails. There was snail ice-cream
for afters.

After supper, Mrs Magic whooshed
everyone up to the Tower.

To her surprise, the children slept
soundly and had sweet dreams.

Chapter Three

The next morning the children were all ready to be scared. Puss told them a real ghost would be serving their breakfast.

Mrs Magic was sure everyone would
have a spooky time on the Spider Train.

Into the darkness they rode...

...to the horrible, hairy heart of
the giant spider's nest.

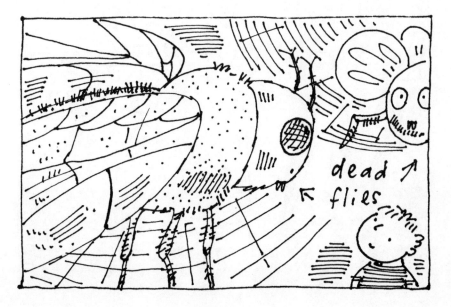

And were they scared? Not one bit.

Mrs Magic was bewildered.

Puss turned the train into a
Curly Wurly Stomach Churner.
And did anyone scream?
Not at all.

Mrs Magic sent all the children to the snake-pit. And do you know what? The snakes were scared of the children.

Chapter Four

Mrs Magic didn't
know what to do.
She couldn't scare
the children.
And the children
grew bored.
Charlie danced
on the roof.

Yoo hoo!

Come down!

Inside the
hotel some
children slid
down the
bannisters.

Others swung from the chandeliers.

Lots of them skated round the hall...

...round the kitchen, into the dining room and round and round the hotel.

The other guests were very upset.

They began to leave. Mrs Magic asked
Puss to do a spell to persuade them
to stay.

Roses are red,
Violets are blue,
The Black Bat Hotel
Is just right for you.

charming

Meanwhile, Mrs Magic wondered what
on earth to do.

Chapter Five

The next morning Mrs Magic held a
meeting with Puss and Partridge.

They searched in the spell books
for a clue.

At last Puss spoke.

So Mrs Magic, Puss and Partridge went for a spin in the Wild Forest. The beasts of the night called to them.

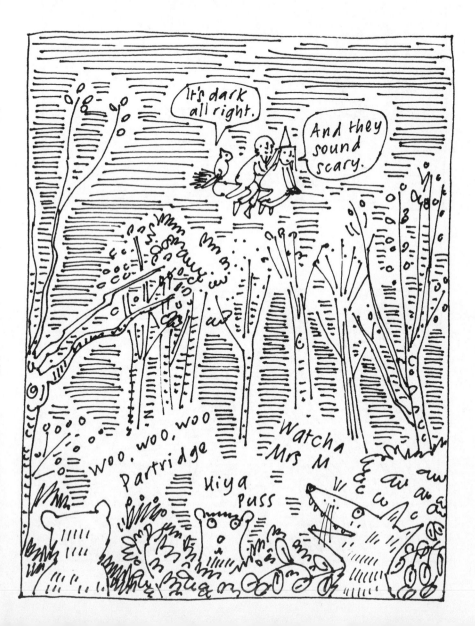

Mrs Magic spoke to the beasts.

The beasts replied.

That night Mrs Magic took the children
for a very special ride. She made
the coach fly high into the sky.

They flew deep, deep into the Wild Forest.
It was very dark indeed.

Suddenly the moon disappeared completely and the beasts of the night cried out.

Puss, who could see in the dark, led everyone out of the coach.

Their knees knocking, teeth chattering,
palms sweating, the children were
terrified at last.

Chapter Six

In the blackest of black, the children were trembling with fear when Puss cast a very unusual spell.

As the moon came out, Puss and
Partridge unpacked a fabulous feast.

One by one the beasts came to join in.
Everyone had a wonderful time.

As dawn broke, the animals went home to sleep.

Mrs Magic was thrilled she had finally found a way to terrify the children.